# WORLD WAR ONE STORIES

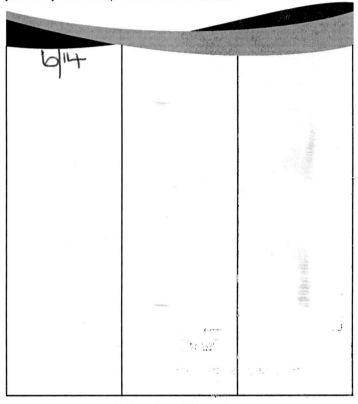

**ISLINGTON**

Please return this item on or before the last date stamped below or you may be liable to overdue charges. To renew an item call the number below, or access the online catalogue at www.islington.gov.uk/libraries. You will need your library membership number and PIN number.

6/14

## Islington Libraries

**020 7527 6900**          **www.islington.gov.uk/libraries**

First published in 2014
by Franklin Watts

Text © Tom and Tony Bradman 2014
Illustrations by Jean-Michel Girard © Franklin Watts 2014
Cover design by Peter Scoulding

Franklin Watts
338 Euston Road
London NW1 3BH

Franklin Watts Australia
Level 17/207 Kent Street
Sydney, NSW 2000

A CIP catalogue record for this book
is available from the British Library.

(pb) ISBN: 978 1 4451 2382 0
(ebook) ISBN: 978 1 4451 2384 4
(Library ebook) ISBN: 978 1 4451 2386 8

1 3 5 7 9 10 8 6 4 2

Printed in Great Britain by CPI Group (UK) Ltd, Croydon, CR0 4YY

Franklin Watts is a division of Hachette Children's Books,
an Hachette UK company.
www.hachette.co.uk

# Contents

# Chapter One
## Seeing Ghosts

Jack Sparkes recognised the place as soon as he saw the battered farm. It was just a few hundred yards down the road. He was marching at the front of the column, next to his mate Bill. The rest of "B" Company was behind them: two hundred soldiers in ranks of four, packs on their backs and rifles slung over their shoulders. It was a warm day and the men sweated inside their thick uniforms. But now Jack felt a sudden chill.

They turned off to march up the dusty track that led to the farm. The order came to fall out and the column broke up, the men sitting in whatever shade they could find. Most of the buildings were more damaged than Jack remembered, the roof of the barn

was gone, its brick walls pitted with bullet-holes, the cow-sheds reduced to heaps of rubble. Amazingly enough the farmhouse itself was still in one piece, and Jack could see it was quickly being transformed into the Company Command Post.

"You all right, Sparky?" said Bill. "You look like you've seen a ghost."

"I'm fine," said Jack with a shrug. "It's just...I've been here before."

"Really?" Bill took off his helmet, pack and rifle and dropped them on the ground, then sat with his back against the wall of the barn. "When was that?"

"I'm not sure." Jack dropped his pack, but kept his helmet on and his rifle slung. "Could have been last year after Fritz's push, or a couple of winters ago..."

The trouble was, of course, that the years had all blurred together. Jack had joined up in 1915 when he'd only been sixteen himself, and he'd hardly been back to Blighty since. He had lived in the Flanders trenches, been shelled and gassed and shot at, fought in battles big and small, and seen hundreds of men die, many here, in this place. So yes, he did feel as if he'd seen a ghost. Lots of them, in fact.

"Oh well, none of it will matter soon," said Bill. He took a swig of water from his canteen and held it out to Jack. "If you ask me we'll all be home by Christmas."

"Is that right?" said Jack. The water was warm and tasted metallic. "If I had a penny for every time I've heard that

old chestnut then I'd be a bloomin'
millionaire."

"But it's different this time. We've
already got Fritz on the run, and who
cares that the Russkies have packed it
in when the Yanks are on our side now?"

Things had certainly changed in 1918, this fourth year of the war. Germany had been fighting on two fronts until late 1917, facing the British and French in the west and Russia in the east. Then the Russian Tsar was toppled by a communist revolution, and the country's new government had signed a peace treaty. So the Germans transferred their eastern armies to the west and launched a huge attack.

It had been touch and go in the early summer. But the British and French had rallied, and for the last two months — it was late August — the Germans had been steadily pushed back. Jack wondered if Bill might have a point about the Americans, who had finally declared war on Germany. But he swiftly crushed the thought. He had seen it all before, and fully expected the Germans to rally in their turn. The last thing he needed was to feel any hope — the war would probably go on forever.

"Sparkes!" somebody yelled. Jack looked up and saw a sergeant at the farmhouse door crooking a finger at him. "You're wanted. Over here, on the double!"

# Chapter Two
## Shrivelled Corpses

Inside the farmhouse Captain Shaw — "B" Company's Commanding Officer — was sitting at the kitchen table studying a large map. "Ah, Corporal Sparkes," he said, looking up. "Little job for you. You're to take a message to our newest allies..."

"Sorry sir, I don't understand," said Jack. An unlikely vision of himself being sent across the Atlantic to meet the American President had popped into his mind.

"We've lost contact with the Americans on our left flank." The captain pointed at the map. "As of yesterday evening they were here, outside this village. Tell them to pull

back and wait until all the support
units have caught up with us."

"I didn't know there were any
Americans around here, sir."

"They're just supposed to fill a

hole in the line, so it's no good them racing ahead without us, if that's what they're doing. Jerry will counterattack into any gap he spots, and I won't let that happen. We'll all move forward when we're ready."

The two men knew each other well. Captain Shaw had been with "B" Company almost as long as Jack. Most of the men at whose side they had fought were dead or wounded, the Company continually being replenished with new blood. Jack's mate Bill had only been called up earlier that year. But the captain was a good officer, one who didn't sacrifice his men unnecessarily. Jack had been impressed by how quickly he had adapted to the new style of warfare of the last few months.

For years the armies on the Western Front had been stuck in trenches. Now they were fighting in the open, the front line constantly changing. At first it had been confusing, but the Army had soon developed new tactics. The infantry moved forward cautiously, probing the German forces with patrols. Attacks were only made when "All Arms" could be brought to bear — artillery barrages to prepare the way, infantry advancing behind tanks, aircraft bombing and strafing enemy positions.

"Righto, sir," said Jack. "Is there anything else you need me to do?"

The captain smiled. "Just take care of yourself — and that's an order."

"Yes, sir!" said Jack, smiling back

and snapping off a crisp salute.

He emerged from the farmhouse, slung his rifle over his back and hurried across the fields, his eyes peeled. The Germans were to the east, but no one was quite sure where. This was familiar territory, though — the village the captain had mentioned was half an hour away by foot. Soon Jack was jumping over a trench "B" Company had once occupied. It was empty now, except for a few shrivelled corpses sinking into the dark, evil-smelling soil. Jack couldn't tell if they were British or German.

Eventually he reached the village. It wasn't as battered as the farm, although there was evidence it had seen some fighting — roofs missing, pockmarked walls, a couple of shell-holes in a street. The Americans — a platoon, maybe sixty men — were resting in a square with houses on four sides. They hadn't posted any lookouts, which would have earned them a roasting from Captain Shaw if he'd been their CO.

In the centre of the square were three Renault FT tanks, made by the French and supplied to the Americans, who had no tanks of their own. They had tiny turrets and stubby guns, and Jack thought they looked like toys compared to the "Land Ironclads", the British Army's heavy tanks.

Each of the Renaults had its engine cowling raised and several men were working on them. Jack wasn't surprised

— Renault FTs had a reputation for breaking down. He was briefly tempted to ask the men if he could give them a hand — he had always loved tinkering

with engines, and before the war he had wanted to be a mechanic. But he walked on, looking for an officer. Then he saw one coming out of a house.

All the Americans were wearing British-style uniforms, the officer's that of a lieutenant. Jack was unsure whether to salute — they might be allies, but they weren't in the same army. He decided to salute anyway. The American simply nodded.

"Urgent message, sir," said Jack. "You're to pull back and wait for support."

"Retreat?" said the officer, frowning. "Hell no — we only just got here!"

# Chapter Three
## Sheer Enthusiasm

"Er...I don't think the order is to retreat exactly, sir, not as such..." Jack replied.

"Pulling back sounds a lot like retreating to me." The American's frown deepened into a scowl. Some of the other Americans were listening now. "It sure isn't going forward, is it? And who is this Captain Shaw guy anyway? Do I know him?"

"He's our Company Commander, sir. We're on your right flank."

"I don't care if he commands the whole British Army. We're soldiers of the 105th Battalion of the US National Guard, and we only take orders from Americans."

"You tell him, Lootenant Sullivan!" a voice yelled, somebody else whistling.

Jack turned and saw a ring of grinning faces, the platoon gathering round. He was struck by how tall and healthy these Americans looked, and how fresh their faces were. He felt curious about them too. Why had that man said "LOOtenant" instead of "LEFFtenant", the way it was pronounced in the British Army? But that wasn't why he'd been sent here. Captain Shaw was depending on him to get his message across.

"I'm sorry, sir," Jack said. "I'm not sure you realise how important this is—"

"Listen, soldier," said the officer. "You guys have spent four years sitting on your butts waiting, and where's that got you? Nowhere. So go back and tell your Captain Shaw to relax. We do things differently. We go forward, don't we, boys?"

"Hell, yeah!" somebody yelled. There was more whistling, even laughter.

Jack scowled now too. He and his mates hadn't exactly been "sitting on their butts" for four years. They had fought and died, struggling on through mud and blood, trying to do their duty and — most important of all — not let each other down. They had also learned the lesson that taking risks was the quickest route to getting killed.

But there was something exciting about the sheer enthusiasm of these Yanks... Besides, Jack and his mates weren't in the trenches any more, they were out in the open where anything might happen. So maybe the "LOOtenant" was right. Maybe they should throw caution to the winds and just get on with it. Jack felt hope fluttering inside him like a young bird taking to the wing...

Just then a soldier ran into the square and up to Lieutenant Sullivan.

"Germans, sir," he said breathlessly. "On the other side of the village!"

The lieutenant smiled. "Gentlemen of the 3rd Platoon, I do believe history beckons. Move out in your squads, like we practised." Then he turned to Jack. "Say, why don't you come along, see how the US Army fights?"

Jack knew he should get back. But

the temptation to see what they could do was too hard to resist.

"Why not?" he said, and followed the lieutenant out of the square.

# Chapter Four
## Good Fighters

The village was bigger than Jack
remembered. Beyond the square was
a wide street, the houses empty,
many with their doors open as if the
inhabitants had left in a hurry. It was
something he had seen a lot over the
last few months, but it still made him
uneasy. There might be snipers lurking
behind some of those windows — which
was why Captain Shaw always sent his
best men ahead to clear them out.

The Americans, however, didn't seem
worried. Back in the square they had
split into five squads of a dozen men
each, but they quickly merged again.
They advanced down the street, a few
looking nervous, most of them clearly

excited and eager to use their rifles. Jack slipped his trusty Lee-Enfield .303 off his shoulder, calmed by the familiar feel of its wooden stock, and checked it had a cartridge up the spout.

"Hey, O'Reilly!" Lieutenant Sullivan called out. "Where are these Germans?"

"Further on a ways, Lieutenant," said the soldier who had reported the sighting. "I saw a couple of them going into a big building. I don't think they saw me."

No, thought Jack, but they could almost certainly hear the platoon heading in their direction. Jack and his mates had learned to be quiet and stealthy when they entered an unknown place, but the Americans

made an incredible amount of noise
— stamping as if they were on a route
march, talking at the tops of their
voices. Captain Shaw would never
have called out to one of his men as
Lieutenant Sullivan had done.

Jack wondered about the two
Germans as well. What were they doing
here? Were they stragglers who had
got separated from their unit? That
happened, but it was unusual, even
in the open warfare of the last few
months. He had a lot of respect for
Jerry. The Germans were good fighters,
their units very disciplined even when
they were retreating. Suddenly Jack
had a nasty feeling that something
wasn't right.

"I see them!" one of the Americans

yelled. "There they are, down the street!"

Several figures dashed across the street a hundred yards ahead, a group of soldiers in field-grey uniforms and coal-scuttle helmets. For a few seconds the Americans stood with their mouths

open, and Jack realised this was probably the first time most had seen the enemy. Then the whole platoon opened fire, the street echoing to the crack of their rifles, rounds whining as they pinged off cobbles and walls.

"After them, men!" yelled the lieutenant, and the platoon surged forward.

"No, wait!" said Jack. But nobody took any notice, so he ran forward too, his eyes on the doorways they passed, the windows, the roofs...

The street ended at the edge of another square, a larger one. The platoon spilled into it and slowed down, looking for the Germans, who had vanished. Jack hung back, scanning the buildings. Three sides were occupied by

cafés, a baker's, houses. The opposite
side was almost entirely occupied by
a big storehouse with brick walls and
a roof of red tiles. It was the building
O'Reilly had talked about, Jack thought.

There had been a line of trees in
front of it, but they had been cut

down — and recently too, judging by the sawdust around the stumps. This gave the building's three windows — all hidden by wooden shutters — a much clearer view of the entire square.

Or a much better field of fire. Jack could almost feel his blood freeze.

"Sir, you need to get your men out of here," he hissed at the lieutenant.

"What are you talking about?" said the lieutenant. "I don't see any—"

The shutters flew open and three machine guns started spitting death.

# Chapter Five
## Utter Madness

Half a dozen men were instantly cut down and the rest dived for any cover they could find. Jack crashed through the door of a nearby café and flung himself on the floor. The windows shattered in a hail of machine-gun rounds, fragments of broken glass bouncing off Jack's helmet and back as he crawled behind the bar and into the café's small kitchen. There he found another door that opened onto an alley.

Jack glanced both ways to make sure the alley was clear, then slipped out. He ran to the point where it joined the street he had come down with the platoon a few moments before. He could still hear the deadly chattering of the machine guns and more glass being shattered. But now there were other sounds as well — the men of the platoon yelling, somebody screaming in terror and pain, the crack of rifle fire.

Jack peered round the corner to find out what was happening and saw the lieutenant doing the same. Sullivan was in another alley on the other side of the street with half a dozen of his men, a pistol in his hand. The Jerry machine-gun fire paused briefly, and Jack took the opportunity to dash across and join the Americans.

"Glad to see you made it," said the lieutenant, nodding. The machine guns opened fire again, and Jack noticed that all the American soldiers ducked, even though none of them were in the field of fire, the bullets striking fiery sparks from the cobbles of the street. All of them, that is, except Lieutenant Sullivan, although he wasn't looking quite as confident as he had done earlier. His face was pale and damp with sweat.

"Er...thank you, sir," said Jack. "I'm sorry, but I really think you should—"

"Save it, will you?" the lieutenant snapped. "I don't have time to talk to you right now. O'Reilly, who got hit? I know Wilson and Ferrara did, but who else?"

There was a brief pause before one of the others spoke. "O'Reilly is dead, sir. He was the first to go down. Leonard and Burke too, and maybe Bergman."

"Goddamit!" said the lieutenant, closing his eyes and shaking his head.

"What are we going to do, sir?" said

another soldier, his voice full of fear.

The lieutenant opened his eyes and looked at them with an expression Jack had seen on the faces of many young officers at such times. It was the moment when everything became very real, when they realised that men's lives depended on their decisions, their leadership. Jack had a feeling that no amount of training could prepare you for such a responsibility. Some men simply couldn't handle it.

Everyone in the alley was staring at the lieutenant, waiting for him to speak. He took a deep breath, visibly getting himself under control, and Jack reluctantly gave him credit for that. The man might be arrogant, but he had guts. Although surely he must come to his senses and obey Captain Shaw's order. All he had to do was round up his men and get the hell out of the village — anything else was utter madness.

"Well, I'll tell you one thing," said the lieutenant. "We're not going to let the Boche hand our butts to us the first time we run up against them. Follow me!"

He moved off, away from the street, and slipped into the rear of another café further down the alley. His men filed in after him. Jack shook his head.

"I don't believe it..." he muttered. Suddenly he heard the dull boom of a grenade exploding. The rifle fire intensified, the machine-gun noise rising to match it.

Jack frowned — and hurried into the café where Sullivan had led his men.

# Chapter Six
## Bullets Buzzing

This café was much larger than the one Jack had escaped into, with a window that gave a wider view of the square. Most of the glass had been shot out, a heavy burst of machine-gun fire disposing of the rest just as Jack emerged from the kitchen. He dived to the floor and crawled forward, his rifle cradled in his arms, pushing past over-turned tables, jagged shards of glass jabbing into his elbows and knees.

Sullivan's men were huddled against the café's front wall, keeping their heads below the level of the window. The lieutenant himself was on one knee beside them, at the corner of the window, peering out across the square.

Jack came up beside him and assumed the same position. Sullivan glanced at him, but said nothing and returned his attention to what was going on outside, so Jack looked out too.

The café was on the right side of the square, at an angle to the building where the machine guns were sited. Each gun was crewed by two German soldiers, one feeding the long cartridge belts into the breech, the other doing the shooting, both protected by layers of sandbags stacked across the bottom of the windows. They were firing steadily, sweeping the whole square, the rounds buzzing like angry metal bees.

Jack could only see three bodies, the men lying where they had fallen,

like bundles of rags dropped from the clear blue sky. The Germans weren't having it all their own way, though. Most of Sullivan's soldiers had taken cover in other buildings on this side

of the square and were firing back, their bullets thumping into the Jerry sandbags, blowing splinters out of the shutters and chunks from the brickwork.

Several Americans had taken shelter behind a small truck, and as Jack watched, one of them lobbed a grenade that exploded with a dull boom. But when the smoke cleared the machine guns were still firing.

"Listen, sir," said Jack, leaning closer to the lieutenant. "I know you don't want to hear this, but you really should pull back before any more of your men get killed."

"Oh yeah?" The lieutenant turned to look at him, his eyes narrowed beneath the rim of his helmet, their faces inches apart. "You're right. I don't want to hear it."

Then he pointed his pistol out of the window and started shooting. His men joined in, all of them rising to their knees and blasting away with their rifles. But that drew the attention of the Germans, the three machine guns now concentrating on the café, streams of bullets filling the air with a storm of steel. Jack hit the floor again.

"Look, you don't understand what you've got yourself into," he yelled at the lieutenant. "You're facing a prepared position. You can try as hard as you like, but you won't flush them out with just a platoon of infantry. You need support."

"We're not giving up yet,"

muttered Sullivan, his face a mask of stubbornness. "Maybe we can go around their flanks, come up behind and surprise them…"

"How do you know there isn't a regiment of Prussian Guards outside the village waiting for you to do just that?" Jack shook his head in exasperation — and came to a decision. "They'll cut you to pieces…but I won't be with you to see it."

He turned and left before Sullivan could say another word.

# Chapter Seven
## Turning Point

The alley behind the café was clear, and Jack carefully made his way back through the village, the sounds of battle loud behind him. He was angry — with the lieutenant for not listening, but also with himself for giving in to the temptation to feel hope again. For a brief moment he had thought the Americans were going to save them all, that their energy and enthusiasm would help to bring this awful war to an end.

But they had let him down, and he didn't want to be there when things got worse, as they were bound to. Jack didn't enjoy abandoning them. The lieutenant and his soldiers were brave, but Jack's clear duty now was to tell

Captain Shaw what was happening.
As the captain had said, Jerry was
brilliant at exploiting even the smallest
weakness, and something like this
could be the turning point of a whole
campaign. Jack had a vision of grey-
uniformed hordes pouring through the
gap in the line...

Just before he arrived at the square
where he had first encountered
the platoon he caught up with two
Americans. One was wounded, the right
leg of his uniform trousers stained dark
with blood, and he was being helped to
hobble along by the other.

"Can I give you a hand?' said Jack,
quickly moving in to support the
wounded man on the other side. He
was clearly in a lot of pain, his face

pale and drawn. The other soldier nodded gratefully, and they struggled on, but only as far as the square.

"I can't make it any further, Earl," said the wounded man. "I got to sit down!"

"All right, Eugene," said Earl. "I ain't sure I can go much further myself..."

The Renault tanks were still in the square, their cowlings still raised. Jack and Earl lowered Eugene into a sitting position, his back against the tracks of one of the tanks.

"I'll have a look at your leg if you like," said Jack. "I've seen lots of wounds."

"Go ahead," Eugene said, his voice shaking. "Just don't make it any worse."

Jack used his bayonet to cut open his trousers. "It's not as bad as it might have been," he said, bandaging the wound with the field dressing he always carried. "The bullet's gone through but it missed the main artery, so you won't bleed to death."

"Thanks, buddy," said Eugene, peering at his leg, the colour returning to his face. "Thanks to you too for getting me out of there, Earl. Thought I was a goner."

"Well, seeing as you ain't, Eugene, I'd better be heading back to the action," said Earl. "Sure wish I could ride in one of those tanks, though. It'd be a lot safer."

Jack looked at Earl more closely. "You were one of the men working on them, weren't you?" he asked. Earl shrugged and nodded. "What's wrong with them?"

"Two are out of gas, and we're a long way from a gas station," said Earl. "The other one just overheated. The radiator is cracked from top to bottom."

An idea began to form in Jack's mind. Something that would help Sullivan and his men, and give Jack time to convince the lieutenant he should follow Captain Shaw's order. Then there wouldn't be a gap in the line, and the Americans wouldn't be wiped out... Of course it was all very chancy — but it was a risk Jack was willing to take.

"If I can get the overheated one going, could you drive it?" he asked Earl.

"You bet," said Earl with a grin. "The French guys gave me a lesson. But if you're thinking of taking out those machine guns, I can't drive and fire the cannon, too."

"Don't worry, mate, I can do that," said Jack. "Right then, let's get started."

It didn't take long. Jack simply swapped the cracked radiator for a good one from a tank without fuel. He

closed the engine cowling and told Earl
to crank up the engine. It roared and a
cloud of thick black smoke belched out
of the Renault's exhaust.

Moments later, Jack and Earl were
heading back towards the battle.

# Chapter Eight
## Powerful Punch

Jack knew the tank was small, of course, but he hadn't realised just how cramped inside it would be. A pair of narrow doors opened at the front so the driver could get to his seat, which took up most of the interior. The gunner had to climb onto the tank and clamber through a small hatch at the back of the turret. He then had to stand in a tight gap behind the driver's seat, his head poking up into the turret.

It was noisy and smelly inside the tank, too. The engine was loud, making it hard for driver and gunner to communicate, and the air they breathed was thick with the smell of petrol. Earl had to wrestle with the levers, too. The tank lurched forward in fits and starts at the pace of a tired snail, its tracks crunching over the cobbles.

But they made it to the square. Earl brought them to a halt by the alley that led to the café where Jack had last seen the lieutenant and his men. Jack peered out of the narrow viewing slit at the front of the turret. Ahead he could see the square and one of the windows in the building opposite, the machine gun still firing steadily. There was a handle to move the turret, and Jack turned it so he could see up the alley.

Lieutenant Sullivan was standing a few feet away, staring at the tank, a look of surprise on his face. Jack turned the turret again and opened the hatch.

"Seeing as you won't pull back and wait for support, I've brought it to you," he said. "You'd better get your men ready to follow up. Can you do that?"

The lieutenant grinned and gave him the thumbs up. Jack pulled the hatch shut and tapped Earl on the shoulder. The tank lurched forward once more, slowly grinding its way out onto the square. The machine guns fell silent for a moment, but then they started up again, concentrating on this new threat. Inside, the Renault's armour began ringing and clanging like a bell in a hailstorm as three streams of bullets hit every part of it.

Jack, however, felt strangely safe in his mobile steel box. About a dozen 37mm shells were clipped around the inside of the turret, each one no longer than his hand. But they were heavy, and Jack had a feeling they would pack a powerful punch. He took one, slipped it into the gun, shut the breech and took aim through the gunsight at the middle window. Then it was simply a question of pulling the trigger...

In less than a minute he demolished almost the entire side of the building, and could see that some of the Germans were fleeing. The Americans were quickly emerging from cover to flush out the rest.

It was good to get out of the tank and breathe fresh air again, even if it was full of brick dust and the bitter smell of cordite from the shells. Earl went off to join his buddies, and Jack stood beside the tank, weary with the usual after-battle fatigue.

"So you just couldn't stay away..." said the lieutenant, coming over to him.

Jack shrugged. "You needed the help, and I knew what to do. Simple, really."

"Yeah, well, I think we should follow up on this, you in that tank and my boys right behind you," said the lieutenant. "We could chase the Germans all the way back to Berlin..." Jack frowned, but Sullivan laughed. "Just kidding. Next time I'll listen to what your Captain Shaw has to say. Then maybe we'll all be home for Christmas."

Jack smiled. He was beginning to think that might actually happen...

# WORLD WAR SHORT STORIES

There are four books to collect!

978 1 4451 2384 4 ebook

978 1 4451 2382 0 pb

978 1 4451 2383 7 ebook

978 1 4451 2381 3 pb

978 1 4451 2390 5 ebook

978 1 4451 2388 2 pb

978 1 4451 2389 9 ebook

978 1 4451 2387 5 pb